This book belongs to:

_____

_____

_____

First Published 2012 by Brown Watson
The Old Mill, 76 Fleckney Road,
Kibworth Beauchamp, Leic LE8 0HG
ISBN: 978-0-7097-2087-4

My Little Book of
Stories for
Girls

Brown Watson

ENGLAND

Dressing Up

Princess Amy and her puppy Scamp
want to play at dressing up.

"Mummy, we need a crown.
Please may we borrow one of yours?
We'll be careful, I promise!"

"We definitely need some jewels,"
says Princess Amy. "There are lots
of lovely necklaces in here."

Amy chooses a pretty necklace
and Scamp carries it into
the playroom.

Then Princess Amy looks in her box of precious things. "I'm sure I have a ring that we can use," she says, shaking the box.

Sharp-eyed Scamp sees a ring that has fallen on the floor. "Well done, Scamp!"

"Now, what else can we find?"
thinks Princess Amy. "Come out of
the toy box, Scamp!"

Princess Amy finds a bag and some
hairclips decorated with daisies.
They're her favourite flower!

Princess Amy runs to find her mummy in the garden. "Whatever is wrong, my dear?" asks her mother.

"Mummy, come quickly! Scamp has got something to show you!"

Princess Amy leads her mummy
to the playroom.

"Look, Mummy!" she giggles.
"We DID play dressing up – and
now Scamp is a princess, too!"

A Secret in the Garden

Princess Ella loves to help in the palace gardens. She puts on her old clothes and even helps with the hard jobs, like digging.

"Gosh, this makes my arms ache!" she says, but she carries on working hard.

The gardener wants her to dig up the dandelions. He says they are weeds. Princess Ella actually likes them. She loves their bright yellow colour.

As she digs, she spots something red amongst the yellow flowers. It's a fairy ring!

Princess Ella checks that no one is watching, and then steps inside the ring.

POOF! Lots of fairies appear in an explosion of sparkling stars. "What do you wish for?" they ask.

What should she wish for? Princess Ella
is a happy girl with lots of luck and
love in her life already.

"I know!" she smiles. "I'd like a dress the
colour of dandelions, please!"

ZAP! In a flash, her wish comes true.

Princess Ella doesn't know whether
to tell anyone about the fairy ring.

"I think I'll keep it a secret," she decides.
"Then nobody greedy or mean can use it to
make bad wishes. And I don't want the
gardener to dig it up!"

Now, whenever Princess Ella wants
somebody to play with or talk to, all she
has to do is go to the fairy ring. Then all
of her new fairy friends come and join
her games at the palace!

Dancing Delight

Princess Grace just loves to dance. She would dance all day if she could. She dances in the fields with her doll, and with all the woodland creatures.

"Oh, Dolly," she smiles. "I wish I could be the best dancer in the whole of this land!"

A passing Pixie hears her wish.
"Then let it be so!" he chuckles, and
casts a magic spell. Princess Grace's
feet begin to tickle and tingle, and
she feels like she could dance with
the wind and skip up to
the stars.

"Come on, Dolly!" she cries. "Let's go!"

Princess Grace is delighted when Dolly begins to dance on her own. They skip and leap along the path side by side. Princess Grace's feet feel like they're flying, and she dances better than she's ever danced before.

Together, Dolly and Princess Grace
dance through the streets. The people
of the town join in, but no one can
keep up for long. Grace is dancing
on air, and soon everyone wants
to watch.

Princess Grace dances on and on, out of the town and through the woods. She doesn't even stop when she reaches a huge muddy puddle. Her magical dancing feet just skip right over the top, without getting dirty.

"Oh, Dolly, I don't ever want to stop dancing! I love it so much!" she cries. "But I am getting tired now. I think it's time to dance home to the palace, and get some rest. Then we can start all over again tomorrow!"

Rainy Days

Princess Alanna wants to play outside,
but it is raining hard. "Oh, toys," she sighs.
"When will the rain ever stop?"

Even Alanna's toys look bored of
being inside all day!

As Princess Alanna wonders what to do,
the sun starts to shine through the window.

"At last!" she cries, leaning out.
"Oh, but it's still raining too." Then she gasps
as a wonderful rainbow appears in the sky.

It looks like the rainbow's end is right in the palace garden. Alanna gathers up her toys and rushes outside to look for it.

"There it is, by the flower bed!" she sings happily.

"Oh – boo!" says Princess Alanna. There is nothing at the end of the rainbow, just a shimmering patch of light. She was hoping for something much more exciting.

She puts down her doll and toy unicorn and wonders if she should play out in the rain anyway.

All of a sudden, Alanna's doll and unicorn spring to life. They grow and grow in front of her eyes, until they are the same size as her.

Princess Alanna claps her hands and jumps onto the unicorn's back. What fun!

"Now I don't want the rain to stop!" laughs
Princess Alanna. After a while, though,
the clouds disappear and the rainbow
fades away.

Princess Alanna's toys shrink back to their
normal size. "Who knows," thinks Alanna.
"Maybe it will rain again soon!"